Books

by Stuart M. Kaminsky

FOUNDED 1830

NEW YORK HOLLYWOOD LONDON TORONTO

SAMUELFRENCH.COM

ISBN 978-0-573-66312-3   Printed in U.S.A.   #4771

IMPORTANT BILLING AND CREDIT
REQUIREMENTS

All producers of *BOOKS* *must* give credit to the Author of the Play in all programs distributed in connection with performances of the Play, and in all instances in which the title of the Play appears for the purposes of advertising, publicizing or otherwise exploiting the Play and/ or a production. The name of the Author *must* appear on a separate line on which no other name appears, immediately following the title and *must* appear in size of type not less than fifty percent of the size of the title type.

CHARACTERS

BRIAN - an incompetent would-be savings and loan robber

MADDY - who runs a less-than-successful used book store along with...

BETTY - who puts up a tough exterior

CHRISTOPHER - a lover of books who can't help stealing them

COP - who is suspicious

ROGER EDMONDS - who is a less-than-successful public defender and an equally inept part-time clown

CLAUDIA - a no-nonsense assistant district attorney

EDDIE - Brian's partner who Claudia never gives a chance to speak

ACT I

Scene I

(The setting is a small used bookstore. Stage left is the entrance. Next to the entrance is a window through which daylight enters. We can see just a bit of that window. There is a book bin in front of the window. Stage right is a counter, behind which is a door leading to the office/ storeroom and washroom. The rear wall facing the audience is covered by book racks filled with books. There is a clock on the wall facing us. The time on the clock is 10:00. There are two wooden chairs beneath the clock for browsers. A wooden ladder is propped against the wall for reaching books on the upper shelves. There are two book bins in the center of the room, one marked "50¢ Each," the other marked "$1 Each." There are books on the counter, perhaps even a few books on one of the chairs under the clock. There is a coffee pot on a hot plate behind the counter.)

(As the play begins we hear a distant wail offstage, a siren. It gradually fades away. On stage are three people: **MADDY**, *about 30, is at the bin near the window, straightening, checking, perhaps marking prices, and occasionally glancing out the window. Her back is to* **CHRISTOPHER**, *probably about 30, dishelved, wearing an overcoat, looking less than savory as he pores over the 50-cent bin books. Behind the counter on a stool sits* **BETTY**, *somewhere in her 40's-50's, reading a book, her glasses perched on the end of her nose. For about 30 seconds,* **BETTY** *drinks and reads,* **CHRISTOPHER** *browses, and* **MADDY** *arranges books at the window.)*

MADDY. "The two women were alone in the London flat."

CHRISTOPHER. Uh, Grahame Greene.

BETTY. No, Doris Lessing, The Golden Notebook.

(She pauses a moment.)

"There was no possibility of taking a walk that day."

MADDY. *(without looking up from her book)* Jane Eyre.

*(Suddenly, from offstage left, outside the window, there is the sound of breaking glass. **MADDY** looks out the window, leaning forward to get a better view.)*

BETTY. *(putting her glasses up on her forehead and placing her book face down on the counter)* What the hell was that?

MADDY. It's across the street. Where Carlo's used to be. The front window it…it just exploded.

*(**BETTY** takes her coffee cup and moves from behind the counter to join **MADDY**. **CHRISTOPHER**, who hasn't moved but has followed the proceedings, waits a beat till he is sure both women are looking out the window. Then, he opens his coat and starts stuffing 50-cent books into the torn lining.)*

BETTY. Exploded? We better call the police.

MADDY. Maybe we should call the fire department.

*(**BETTY** turns quickly toward the counter almost catching **CHRISTOPHER** in his theft. He plunges his hands into his coat pocket and says:)*

CHRISTOPHER. The fire department. Definitely the fire department.

MADDY. *(Still looking out the window)* Hold it. Someone's coming out. I think he's hurt.

*(**BETTY** turns back to the window. Since **BETTY** and **MADDY** are not listening to him or watching him, **CHRISTOPHER** pinches a few more books.)*

BETTY. You're right. He's hurt.

MADDY. We've got to help him.

*(**MADDY** goes to the door and opens it. Outside, she shouts:)*

Here, come over here.

*(We can't see **MADDY** outside for a few seconds. Then she enters helping **BRIAN** who is about 35 or 40 wearing a light jacket and jeans. In one hand he carries a YMCA gym bag. His face is bleeding from a cut on his forehead. There is a red Band-Aid on his cheek. As **BETTY** enters looking concerned, **BRIAN** slams the door shut and leans back against is panting.)*

BRIAN. Oh, Jesus, oh Jesus. Oh Christ. There is just so much goddamn irony a person can take in this life.

(looking at them)

I mean you plan, work things out, details, touches. This Band-Aid.

(He rips off the Band-Aid to reveal nothing. He throws the Band-Aid away.)

CHRISTOPHER. I don't see…

BRIAN. Right. You got it. You wear a Band-Aid and people don't remember your face, just the Band-Aid. Little details.

CHRISTOPHER. Why didn't you put the Band-Aid on the real cut?

BRIAN. What's the matter with you? Did you hear what I'm saying here?

*(**BETTY** leads **BRIAN** to one of the chairs. **MADDY** has hurried behind the counter and is looking for a towel in the washroom offstage. She returns while **BRIAN** speaks and hands the towel to **BETTY** who begins to take care of his cut.)*

BRIAN. No matter what you do, you deserve some dignity, some sense of meaning, accomplishment, right?

BETTY. *(absently, assuming he is ranting)* Right.

CHRISTOPHER. *(seriously)* Right.

BRIAN. You know that store across the street? I was so damned careful. Cool, I was as cool as…as…that guy on television, you know? The guy who sells oatmeal and…and…diabetes stuff?

CHRISTOPHER. Wilford Brimley. Did you know he was in *The Thing*? The remake not the original?

BRIAN. *(ignoring him)* For Chrissake. I rented the place a month ago, told the landlord we were going to reopen it.

CHRISTOPHER. Deep-dish pizzas? I'd buy one, but you picked the wrong neighborhood. This one's closing up and moving out.

BRIAN. *(while* **BETTY** *stops the bleeding)* It was Eddie's fault. For Chrissake, it was his fault. There was no damned good reason why I should hold his gun. Mine wasn't even loaded and, boom, it goes off in there *(nods across the street),* blows the window out, ruins the whole damn thing.

MADDY. Guns?

CHISTOPHER. Sounds like it was your fault for working with this Eddie.

BRIAN. *(looks up at* **CHRISTOPHER** *menacingly, changes his mind and, then looks dejected)* Maybe you're right. I planned it. The little details. The bag, the jogging costume for him under his suit. The Band-Aid. Did I say the Band-Aid?

BETTY. We better get you to a doctor and we'd better call the police about the window. It could be dangerous.

CHRISTOPHER. *(reminds her)* The fire department.

(MADDY nods and moves toward the phone. BRIAN watches her dully as she goes behind the counter, picks it up and starts thumbing through a phone book. BRIAN realizes what is happening and perks up.)

MADDY. You'll be fine. We'll clean up that cut and get you over to the emergency room at St. Gervais.

BRIAN. No.

BETTY. You may need stitches. The fireman can…

BRIAN. *(standing and pulling a pistol from his pocket)* No. Put the phone down.

MADDY. Oh, God.

(She puts the phone down.)

BETTY. *(backing away from* **BRIAN** *and moving near* **CHRISTOPHER** *who has backed away)* What the hell are you doing?

BRIAN. I don't know. Jesus God. I don't know. I've got to think. Don't push me.

CHRISTOPHER. Let the man think.

BRIAN. *(taps the barrel of the pistol against his head and looks back at the clock)* An hour, a whole hour.

(He looks out the window.)

CHRISTOPHER. Can I ask you a question?

BRIAN. *(thinking)* What?

CHRISTOPHER. Is that your gun or your friend Eddie's?

BRIAN. *(looks at the gun.)* Mine...No, it's Eddie's. How many customers you expect this morning? What's usual?

*(***MADDY** *and* **BETTY** *speak at the same time:)*

BETTY. Dozens.　　　　　**MADDY.** None.

BRIAN. *(holding his gun high and looking at the ceiling)* This is goddamn hard for me. Just tell me the truth and maybe we can all walk out of here.

BETTY. We probably won't have any customers, maybe a stray or who knows? This isn't exactly Barnes and Noble.

BRIAN. Good.

BETTY. That depends on who you are and what you want. What do you want?

BRIAN. We're all going to wait for Eddie. Eddie's supposed to meet me back at the store at 11. We were going to hole up there for a day or two. We'll just wait here for Eddie and catch him before he goes in.

MADDY. What's this all about?

BRIAN. The Second Federal Savings and Loan was robbed about fifteen minutes ago.

CHRISTOPHER. And you want us to guess who did it?

BRIAN. I did it. Eddie and I did it. It was perfect, a thing of beauty…

CHRISTOPHER. …and a joy until ten o'clock.

BRIAN. *(quickly, menacingly)* I told you there is just so much irony a person can take. And I'm up to my ass in it now.

BETTY. You plan to keep us all here till this Eddie shows up.

*(**BRIAN** nods.)*

MADDY. Then what?

BRIAN. Then…then we'll think of something.

BETTY. That's a good plan.

BRIAN. You have a better one? You want me to just take my bag and go running down the street waving my gun? Should I go out there and shoot it out with the cops?

BETTY. I assume you aren't really asking.

BRIAN. *(aervous, mocking)* You ah-summe right, lady.

BETTY. Then I can assume that we are hostages.

BRIAN. No, no, no. You are not hostages. I'm unequivocally not taking hostages. I'm covering my ass here. You are not hostages. I'm just asking the three of you to go on about your business while I wait for a friend and maybe look at some books. I'll even buy a few books.

CHRISTOPHER. *(taking a tentative step towards the door)* I can go?

BRIAN. This gun went off once today beyond my control. It might happen again. It wouldn't be my fault.

CHRISTOPHER. I'll browse a little while longer.

MADDY. *(giggles, the start of hysteria)* I can't take this for an hour.

BETTY. Maddy, he'll put the gun away and sit quietly. We'll just go on with the inventory.

*(She looks at **BRIAN**, who gives a "what-the-hell" shrug and puts the gun in his belt.)*

BRIAN. It can come back out fast, remember that.

BETTY. O.K., Wild Bill, just have a seat and let's make this as painless as possible.

BRIAN. Lady, I don't think I like you.

BETTY. I'm probably not at my best today.

BRIAN. Just keep your smart-ass talk to yourself, lady. You want your store in one piece, you'll just shut up and leave me alone.

BETTY. It's not my store. It's hers. I just work here.

BRIAN. What're your names?

BETTY. Why?

BRIAN. I don't know. I read in a book once you use people's first name they think you're not going to hurt them, make it personal, you know?

CHRISTOPHER. Robert Duvall did that in that old movie *The Outfit.*

BETTY. Very reassuring.

BRIAN. I don't like smart asses.

BETTY. And I don't like dirty ones.

MADDY. *(warning)* Betty, please for God's sake.

BRIAN. You some kind of mass-o-chist? You looking to get hurt?

BETTY. *(putting her hand to her head and sighing.)* You may find this hard to believe, Mister Whatever-your-name is...

BRIAN. Brian...shit, Forget I told you my name. Forget. What the hell's the matter with me. It's this day.

BETTY. *(continuing)* You may find this hard to believe, but there are things more important than you on my mind. Don't get me wrong. You are a significant factor at the moment, but in an hour you'll be resolved. You'll walk out of here or...

CHRISTOPHER. He'll walk out of here.

BETTY. *(She shrugs and goes to pour herself another coffee.)* All right. You'll walk out of here and I'll still have things to worry about.

BRIAN. What the hell are you talking about, things to worry about?

MADDY. Betty's waiting to hear from the doctor about some tests. She...she may have...

BETTY. Maddy, Brian has his own business to take care of.

BRIAN. *(looking out of the window as he has been from time to time all through the scene)* I'm sorry, but we all gotta go...

BETTY. *(pausing as she pours coffee, emphatically but softly)* Don't say it. Don't finish saying it or so help me, gun or no gun, I'll throw this coffee in your face.

BRIAN. Can I have some of that coffee?

BETTY. *(shrugs and hands the cup to* **MADDY** *who brings it to him.)* You've got the money in that bag, haven't you?

BRIAN. Right. And I haven't even had a chance to count it, but there's a lot in there, a lot.

CHRISTOPHER. What are you going to do with it?

BRIAN. *(incredulously)* Give it to the homeless...Hell, I'm going to spend it. If anyone comes through that door, let them buy a book and keep everything normal.

MADDY. Why don't we just close up?

BRIAN. Use your toochis, lady. It might look funny if you close when you're supposed to be open and what are we supposed to do, hide behind the counter?

(He takes a pair of books from a shelf and put them on his lap.)

If someone comes in I'll open this book and pretend I'm reading it, but just you remember, I won't be reading it.

BETTY. Will you be looking at the pictures?

BRIAN. Lady, you don't know from square one about me but you're full of cracks about how dumb I must be. How smart are you with all these books? They going to keep you alive five minutes longer? They going to make dying easier?

BETTY. Yes to both questions.

BRIAN. Jesus, I forgot...I'm sor...

CHRISTOPHER. *(jumping in, to* **MADDY***)* This is like *No Exit*. *(to* **BRIAN***)* That's a play by...

BRIAN. Jean Paul Sartre. I saw the movie on TV. It stinks. I didn't say I can't read. I learn a new word every day, every day. A strong body and a vocabulary, that gets you respect.

CHRISTOPHER. What's your word for today?

BRIAN. *(glancing at the window, sarcastically)* I haven't had time. Yesterday's was "regurgitate." How many guys in my line you think can use words like "unequivocally" and "masochist" and "regurgitate??"

CHRISTOPHER. Your line?

BRIAN. *(to BETTY)* Robber. I don't hide from the people I take from. I take 'em face to face.

BETTY. I'm sure they appreciate that.

BRIAN. I don't do it for them. It's for me.

CHRISTOPHER. Admirable. A thief with a strong neck and a vocabulary.

BRIAN. I'm a robber. You're a thief. *(to BETTY)* Look at that coat in this weather. Look at the way it sags. He must have seven or eight of your books in the lining.

CHRISTOPHER. *(looks panicked and backs away.)* I've gotta use the toilet.

BRIAN. *(warning)* No one leaves this room.

BETTY. There aren't any windows or doors in the toilet. Take a look.

BRIAN. All right. All right. All right. Go in there and play with yourself. Just don't take long.

*(**CHRISTOPHER** moves behind the counter and goes through the door closing in behind him.)*

MADDY. *(pouring a cup of coffee)* He does not have seven or eight books in his coat. He has exactly eleven books, all from the 50-cent table. That's five dollars and fifty cents. If you like I can give you the titles. He comes in every week and we pretend we don't see what he doing. He sneaks out and his brother comes in on Saturday and pays for everything he's taken. Actually, he's one of out best customers. What's more he reads all the books he takes.

BRIAN. He's feeble minded.

BETTY. He is literate and burned out from too many trips to the hospital for depression, too many pills, too many treatments, too many...

BRIAN. Great. I stumbled into an episode of *The Young and the Restless.*

BETTY. No, you pushed your way in.

BRIAN. You invited me. Remember that if it comes to it. You invited me in here.

(There is a flushing sound from offstage right.)

BRIAN. *(glancing down at the books on his lap)* Slave Girls of the Kalahari.

(looks at second book)

William Blake. He was crazy, wasn't he?

MADDY. Why don't you read him and make up your own mind?

BRIAN. O.K. How much is this book?

MADDY. You can have it.

BRIAN. I pay my way lady.

BETTY. With someone else's money.

BRIAN. Now wait a minute. Banks, savings and loans, they're...

BETTY. Hold it. You can keep us in here with your gun but I don't think I can keep up the pretense of conversation with you if you're going to give us worn out crap about how banks are insured and nobody loses. I saw *Bonnie and Clyde.* I could take it from Warren Beatty, but you're no Warren Beatty.

BRIAN. Johanna, my ex-wife, thought I looked like James Caan.

BETTY. She lied.

BRIAN. Not the face. I've got hair all over my body.

BETTY. Fascinating.

BRIAN. You're being smart-assed again, aren't you?

MADDY. *(nervous, angry, drinking her coffee)* Why don't you leave her alone, leave us alone? Just, sit there and read the book and don't wave your damn gun around and shut up, shut up, shut up.

BRIAN. Calm down. I don't want anyone to look in and see you going crazy. What the hell's this all about? Why are you acting like this?

BETTY. I can't imagine.

BRIAN. And what's he doing in the john so long? How long does it take? You sure there's no window, nothing in there?

BETTY. There's no window, nothing, just a toilet, a sink and an empty safe.

BRIAN. *(gets up and walks toward the bathroom door, then calls out)* Hey you, in there. What's his name?

MADDY. Christopher.

BRIAN. Christopher. Get your ass out here. We all know what you're doing. You're in there with the books you jacked and you're playing with yourself.

CHRISTOPHER. *(from inside)* No such of a thing.

BRIAN. You've got a minute to get out here. Make that fifteen seconds.

(A flashing light comes through the bookstore window. BRIAN turns. The light falls on him eerily.)

Shit.

MADDY. *(looking out of the window, near hysteria)* What did you expect? The window's broken. There's glass all over the street. Someone called them.

(MADDY and BRIAN look out the window. BETTY glances out and then walks slowly behind the counter, takes a sip of her coffee, looks at the phone and then sits back on her stool.)

BRIAN. He's going in through the window. What's the other cop doing? I can't see him?

MADDY. *(who has moved to a corner and is looking down the street)* He's looking in the other windows. The bakery... Now I can't see him.

BRIAN. The cop's coming out of the window.

BETTY. I really appreciate the play-by-play. It makes things clear for those of us who are blind.

BRIAN. Oh shit. He's coming this way. I think he's coming here. He's looking at the ground.

MADDY. Blood. He's following the trail of blood from your cut.

BRIAN. No, oh ma, no. Why me. Oh ma, why me. Why not Eddie. It was all his fault. It isn't fair. God, why me.

BETTY. I admire your grace under pressure.

MADDY. Betty, we could all get shot.

    (**BETTY** *shrugs.*)

BRIAN. He's looking here.

    (*goes back to the chair and sits*)

Remember, I've got this gun.

    (*He tucks the gun away and picks up the book. As we see the face of the cop at the window.*)

And remember, you're not hostages.

    (*The cop enters.* **MADDY** *is nervously pretending to arrange books.* **BETTY** *looks up at the cop and over at* **BRIAN** *who gives her a warning glance.*)

COP. What happened over there?

    (*He looks at* **BRIAN** *whose face is buried in the book.*)

MADDY. The window broke. I think some kids threw a rock at the window.

COP. I didn't see no rock and the glass is all over the sidewalk and street. Looks like something broke it from inside. Who got hurt?

MADDY. Hurt?

COP. There's blood leading right to your door.

    (*To* **BRIAN**, *seeing his bandage.*)

You got hurt. What do you know about that window?

BETTY. He was walking past when it broke. Maddy saw him and he came over here. I put bandage on it.

COP. You see anyone over there.

BRIAN. No.

COP. Where were you heading?

(**COP** *glances at his bag.*)

BRIAN. The Y. I lift weights.

COP. The Y's maybe 15 blocks from here.

BRIAN. Good exercise. Warms me up.

COP. You live around here?

BRIAN. Yeah, over on…What's going on?

COP. Federal Savings and Loan over on Sixth was held up maybe half an hour ago. We got the call on this window business. Dispatch sergeant thought there might be a connection.

BRIAN. No connection.

COP. How do you know?

BRIAN. I don't. I'm a little mixed up, my head.

COP. Let's get you over to the Emergency Room, have that head looked at.

BRIAN. No.

MADDY. (*at the same time*) Yes.

BETTY. (*after a menacing look from* **BRIAN**) Eddie will be here in few minutes to take him.

BRIAN. Eddie's my partner. We called him a few minutes ago.

COP. Why didn't you call in about the window being broke?

MADDY. Our phone is out of order.

(*phone rings*)

It's fixed.

BETTY. (*grabs the phone, sighs, and says:*) Book Haven. Yes, this is she.

(*She turns on her stool.* **MADDY** *looks at her with concern. The cop speaks up and we cannot hear* **BETTY**'s *conversation.*)

COP. (*to* **MADDY**) You see anything unusual out there in the last hour? Any strangers, you know, anything like that, even a cat, something?

BRIAN. No, nothing.

MADDY. Nothing.

(**COP** *looks at* **BRIAN** *again who has turned back to his book.*)

BETTY. *(her voice low, still on the phone.)* I see. Yes. Of course I will…

(*The* **COP** *is about to leave after looking over his shoulder at the street when we hear the distinct and quite loud sound of a toilet flushing.* **COP** *turns to the washroom door.* **CHRISTOPHER** *emerges, seeing the* **COP**. *He holds his hands out and moves to the bin a few feet from the* **COP**. *Without a word he starts pulling paperbacks out of his coat pockets, dozens of them, a regular Harpo Marx collection, and puts them back into the bin. Just when we think he is finished, he finds more. This ends with the turning up of a rather sizeable hardcover book.*)

COP. What the hell is this?

MADDY. About five times as much as I thought he had.

CHRISTOPHER. I just took them in to look at in the washroom. You don't want to arrest me for that, a few books. What about him?

(*points to* **BRIAN**.)

COP. What about him?

BRIAN. *(hand on his gun)* What about me?

CHRISTOPHER. He…he…he…

MADDY. … needs medical attention.

CHRISTOPHER. Right.

BRIAN. Eddie's coming for me. You were in the john when we called Eddie.

COP. How could you call Eddie if the phone wasn't working? You just told me the phone was broken until a minute ago.

BRIAN. Maddy went out and called. Where did you call from, Maddy?

MADDY. *(confused)* Where did I call…*(vaguely)* The corner.

COP. Forget it. Now that the phone's fixed call in if you see anyone suspicious. You ask me the guys who took the

Federal are somewhere in Indiana by now.

(*nods at* **CHRISTOPHER** *and speaks to* **MADDY**)

You want me to take him out of here?

(**MADDY** *is about to speak when* **BRIAN** *interrupts.*)

BRIAN. No, please, Officer. He's harmless, a neighborhood character. We all kind of look after him. Right, Maddy?

MADDY. Right.

CHRISTOPHER. Hey, wait a minute here. You're talking about me like I'm some kind of half-wit. I've read more than all of you.

MADDY. And pays less to do it.

COP. (*glances out window*) I've gotta get going.

(*And out he goes.*)

BETTY. (*ending her phone conversation*) Yes, thank you.

(*She hangs up, looks around.*)

A very perceptive policeman.

BRIAN. You're lucky he wasn't more perceptive.

BETTY. (*laughs bitterly*) Lucky.

MADDY. Was that Dr. Forbes on the phone?

BETTY. It was.

MADDY. And?

BETTY. And, surgery Monday. There's a tumor.

(*looks placidly at* **BRIAN**.)

So who has the troubles, Bank Robber?

BRIAN. (*uneasy*) My sister had a tumor. They took it out and she was home in a day. Benign. Odds are yours is too.

BETTY. It wasn't last time.

MADDY. Betty, oh Betty.

BRIAN. (*embarrassed, scratches his head and looks out the window*) What're they looking at? Why are those cops looking back here?

CHRISTOPHER. We piqued their interest.

(He too looks out the window and waves.)

They're going now. They have reached their peak and are now descending.

BRIAN. Maybe they think something's wrong here.

BETTY. What could possibly give them that idea?

BRIAN. Listen, Lady, I'm sorry about your, your tumor. You'll go to the hospital. They'll take care of you. My problem is right now, now, here.

BETTY. I had no choice about my problem, Bank Robber, you did. No one in here is going to feel sorry for you. And I don't want anyone feeling sorry for me. I can handle that myself, thank you.

BRIAN. O.K. I don't feel sorry for you. You seem like a gutsy...

BETTY. You say "broad" and you'll have a faceful of coffee, gun or no gun.

CHRISTOPHER. *The Big Heat.* Lee Marvin did it to Gloria Grahame in *The Big Heat.* Coffee right in her face. Uggh.

BRIAN. I haven't had it all that easy here lady. Let me tell you. You got a regular job. You eat regular. You talk like college.

BETTY. If you're going to tell us your life story, I'd rather be shot.

BRIAN. My father...my father was a cab driver.

(The memory has obviously touched him. He pauses waiting for a reaction.)

BETTY. We, and I think I can use that editorially, do not give a damn.

BRIAN. You don't, huh? What if I told you my father was blind?

CHRISTOPHER. A blind cab driver? You're from New York.

BRIAN. No, no. I mean what if I had told you that, that my father was blind. You'd have been all sympathy. Poor kid, that kind of shit, right?

MADDY. No.

BRIAN. *(trying another ploy)* It was my mother who was blind.

MADDY. I don't believe you.

BETTY. I don't care.

CHRISTOPHER. Prove it. Show us some sign language.

BRIAN. That's deaf people.

MADDY. I still don't believe you and what difference does it make?

BRIAN. I'm trying to give things perspective, make them personal, you know.

CHRISTOPHER. Like using out first names, right, Brian?

BRIAN. Something like that. What's your story... ?

CHRISTOPHER. Guido.

BRIAN. Your name isn't Guido. It's...don't shit me, man. Christopher, it's Christopher. I'm trying to be regular with you and you're shitting me.

BETTY. If you want to be amused, read one of the books behind you, or pull out your gun and make us dance. We can do without your grotesquerie.

BRIAN. *(mock admiration)* Grow-tesk-query. You know what you are, what I am? A few years of nothing kept alive with an idea that maybe we're more. But we ain't. What do your books say about that?

BETTY. You wouldn't understand.

BRIAN. If I'm wrong, tell me how in easy words. Am I wrong?

BETTY. *(a sigh)* Maybe not.

(Everyone is silent.)

*(**CHRISTOPHER** steps forward. **BRIAN** shows his gun. **CHRISTOPHER** holds out his hands and points at the book in **BRIAN**'s lap. **BRIAN** tosses it to him. **CHRISTO-PHER** flips through it, finds what he is looking for and reads.)*

CHRISTOPHER. I always take my judgment from a Fool Because his judgment is so very Cool Nor prejudiced by feelings great or small Amiable State he cannot feel at all.

(closes the book and hands it back)

*(***BRIAN*** throws the book at ***CHRISTOPHER****, gets up and punches ****CHRISTOPHER****, knocking him down.* ***BETTY*** *watches with arms folded as* ***MADDY*** *runs forward and pushes* ***BRIAN*** *away as he is about to kick the fallen* ***CHRISTOPHER****.* ***BRIAN*** *pulls his arm back as if to hit her,* ***CHRISTOPHER*** *writhes on the floor.)*

BETTY. *(cooly)* Have you ever shot anyone, Bank Robber?

*(***BRIAN*** *hesitates, looks at her as* ***MADDY*** *kneels to help* ***CHRISTOPHER****.)*

BRIAN. I'm in no goddamn mood.

(moves in front of ***MADDY****)*

BETTY. We can see that. But if you touch her, you're going to have to kill me. You ready for that?

BRIAN. *(shouting)* What do you know? I mean what the… What do you know? No, I never shot anyone. Shit, I only pulled a trigger once and blew out that goddamn window. I'm a hold-up man and if you have to know I haven't been all that damned good at it. In fact if you have to know, I've been shitty at it, but this bag is full. You don't want my life story, fine. I don't want yours either lady. I don't know you people. You live in books, goddamn books. Other people's ideas, words, stories. You sit in here all day letting your lives go by. I may be a damn failure, but I'm out there on the streets living.

BETTY. You don't know what we are. You see three people in a book store who needle you because you come here with a runty gun, a temper, and a Reader's Digest vocabulary certificate, and you pull out your story about how anybody who went past the eighth grade doesn't know about life. Brian, you know what your trouble is?

MADDY. *(helping* ***CHRISTOPHER****, now bloody, to sit up)* Betty, let it be.

BRIAN. No, but I got a feeling you're gonna tell me.

BETTY. You're living on a bloated little ego stretched as far as it can go. You're a puny little balloon about to explode and when you do a little puff of hot air will come out whimpering, "me, me, me."

BRIAN. I think I'm ready to do some killing.

(He pulls out his pistol.)

MADDY. Stop it. For Christ's sake Betty, stop it. If you want to commit suicide, do it somewhere else, not here. I don't want to go with you.

CHRISTOPHER. *(with a cough)* And besides we're having so much fun.

(coughs again)

BRIAN. *(rubbing his forehead)* Goddamn You! Hear what I'm saying? Goddamn.

(He puts his pistol away, picks up his YMCA bag, sits down with it in his lap and clutches it to his chest, glaring angrily at them all.)

If Eddie doesn't come in five minutes, I'm getting out of here.

BETTY. You going to kill us and leave no witnesses.

MADDY. Betty.

BRIAN. Leave me alone. I'm not killing anyone. You're not hostages, remember? I'll...I'll tie you up or lock you in the john. Shut up and let me think, goddamn you. Shut up.

CHRISTOPHER. *(helped up by MADDY, leans against the counter)* Let Duke Mantee think. It will be a refreshing change. Even at the rudimentary level of his cognition it will be better than having him act.

BRIAN. *(pulls out his gun and fires into the ceiling)* Oh shit. Look what you made me do? Oh shit.

(He gets up and looks out the window, back and forth.)

No one there. Upstairs. Who lives upstairs?

(He is waving his gun frantically.)

MADDY. No one. It's just storage space.

BRIAN. Look what you people made me do. Have I ever done anything to you? I didn't rob you did I? I just want to get the hell out of here with this bag. Why are you on me? You people are always on me, people you look down on. I eat, screw, shit and bleed just like you do.

BETTY. Three out of four ain't bad, Shylock. I hope that number two veiled sexual suggestion.

BRIAN. Not hardly, lady. I've got better waiting for me.

BETTY. That's a relief.

BRIAN. *(fighting back)* I don't make it with broads who are dying.

BETTY. You do have a way with words, haven't you?

BRIAN. You just irk me is all. I didn't mean that.

BETTY. I prefer thinking you did mean it.

MADDY. I can't take anymore of this. I want you *(to* **BRIAN***)* to get out. Get out. Take your gun and your money and get out.

BRIAN. *(looks around at each of them)* That's it. You got it. I'm going. I don't want to put in another minute with you three. It's like a year in the slam. I'm going. Get your asses in the john. Get in there. Get in there. You back me up and what choice am I gonna have here?

BETTY. *(calmly)* No.

MADDY. Yes.

CHRISTOPHER. I think…no.

> *(As* **BRIAN,** *tears in his eyes, raises his gun and aims at* **BETTY,** *the phone rings. They look at each other and* **BRIAN** *says with a deep sigh:)*

BRIAN. O.K. Answer it. Answer it.

MADDY. *(answering)* Hello. Book Haven…yes…I…yes, he is.

> *(She turns to* **BRIAN** *and holds out the phone.)*

It's for you.

> *(CURTAIN)*

Scene Two

(Same location. The act begins where the last one ended. The clock is at the same time. **BRIAN** *takes the phone.)*

BRIAN. *(on phone)* Eddie, where are you? No, wait, I got a better question. How did you know I was here?

(Long pause while **BRIAN** *listens. His face goes through several changes. In order, they are shock, despair, agony. He ends with a bit of defiant anger and self pity. Without another word,* **BRIAN** *hangs up the phone, walks to the window, looks both ways, touches his gun and goes back to the chair. Instead of sitting in it, he moves it to the door of the shop, props it against the knob and turns the sign to show "closed" to the outside. He then sits in the other chair, eyes on the door, brooding.)*

BETTY. Well, are you going to let us in on it or do we have to guess?

(The look **BRIAN** *gives her prompts* **MADDY** *to say…)*

MADDY. Let's just guess.

CHRISTOPHER. *(feeling for broken bones)* I'd say the police picked up his friend and his friend promptly turned him in.

MADDY. But how did they know he was here?

CHRISTOPHER. *(shrugs)* They just guessed.

BRIAN. *(without looking away from the door)* The cop. The cop who was in here. When they brought Eddie in and he told about the store, they checked with the cop who came here to look at the broken window. He remembered me saying I was waiting for Eddie. He didn't look that bright.

MADDY. And they're out there?

*(***BRIAN*** nods rubbing his face with his free hand.)*

I don't see anyone, just a…yes, there.

BRIAN. They gave me fifteen minutes to throw out the gun and come out. If I don't come, the street will be filled

with cops. There's probably a sniper over on that goddamn roof over the store. Eddie, Eddie, Eddie, Eddie.

MADDY. How'd you like a cup of coffee before you go out?

BRIAN. I've gotta think.

BETTY. What's there to think about? If you don't go out
there, they shoot you. Seems pretty straightforward to
me. A nice simple either/or.

BRIAN. Nice and simple. You ever been in the slam, any of
you?

*(He expects a "no" from everyone with the possible excep-
tion of **CHRISTOPHER** and is surprised by…)*

MADDY. I did nine months in Corona in 2004.

*(**BRIAN** and **CHRISTOPHER** are taken aback. **BETTY**
knows all about it.)*

I was twenty. My boyfriend and I were drunk. We stole
a car and hit an old man. He lived but…

BRIAN. Felony One. And you, high pockets. You ever do
time or did that brother of yours buy you clean? Hell,
no one spends time for shoplifting. How did you like
the prison, Miss Lonelyhearts?

MADDY. The time was so slow. It…a day wouldn't end and
there were women in there who…the books kept me
from going crazy. That's why I opened this shop.

BRIAN. I'm no reader. I didn't even have that. And I get this
thing in my chest. This wound up thing that makes my
heart go crazy at night in the dark and I panic. Then I
want out and there's no out. You know that feeling?

*(**BRIAN** has been pacing furiously, glancing from time to
time out the window.)*

MADDY. Yes.

BETTY. We all know it. Maybe that's why we don't rob
banks.

BRIAN. It was a Savings and Loan, not a bank and it was
my first. I don't know. You get into a thing and you
don't see any other way. It's like you got no choices.

It's gonna happen. Eddie tells me about the job and I don't even think about it. I just go.

CHRISTOPHER. I thought you said the robbery was your idea.

BRIAN. *(Sagging, scratching his head with his gun.)* It was Eddie's. You wanna hear something?

BETTY. No.

BRIAN. Nothing was my idea. I don't have ideas. It was all Eddie's idea, even the Band-Aid on my cheek. Hell, I get caught whenever I listen to somebody else and I can't stop listening. I can't stop. You understand that?

*(**MADDY** goes cautiously to the window to look for the police. **CHRISTOPHER** staggers toward the bathroom.)*

Hey, where are you going?

CHRISTOPHER. To wash my bloody face and soothe my savaged ribs. You wanna kick my a few times before I go. It might save me a trip later.

BRIAN. *(disgusted)* Go on.

*(**CHRISTOPHER** goes to the washroom and closes the door.)*

BETTY. Let's look at this. Staying in here doesn't give you anything and there's only one way out. I don't think you're giving serious consideration to going out shooting.

BRIAN. *(looking up at her seriously)* Like Paul Muni or Al Pacino in Scarface or Cagney in White Heat, or your pal Beatty in Bonnie and Clyde, or...

BETTY. You've thought about it.

BRIAN. *(touching the YMCA bag)* I could've been a winner today. I walk out that door with my hands in the air and I'm nothing. But I walk out shooting and I'm right behind the lotto jackpot on the six o'clock news. I got a chance to pick my time.

BETTY. You've got a point bank robber, but when the time comes, you'll tell yourself its better to have a few more years or weeks or minutes. I've been through that door.

BRIAN. Thanks.

(There is the sound of running water in the washroom. It stops. The door is open.)

MADDY. I don't see anyone on the roof.

BRIAN. You're not supposed to.

(looks over shoulder at the clock)

So, I got to face it. I'm a zero here. I throw down the gun, walk out, get slammed and maybe live long enough to come out an old man and die a nothing. That's the score.

BETTY. *(shrugging)* If you're lucky.

BRIAN. You think you…you know, come back after you're dead, have a soul, that kind of thing? If I knew that, hell, I could go right out there like Butch and Sundance. What do your books say?

BETTY. Anything you want them to say.

BRIAN. And what do you think?

BETTY. I'll let you know when I find out, which may be soon.

MADDY. Stop it. Damn you stop that. What are you trying to do to me?

BETTY. To you? Maddy I wasn't thinking about you.

BRIAN. See what I mean? No one thinks about anybody else, just themselves. Shut up. I've got to think here.

(BRIAN *looks nervously at the clock and out the window.)*

CHRISTOPHER. *(coming out of the washroom gargling)* Grrrrrrrrgh.

BRIAN. What the…get back in there. You're disgusting.

CHRISTOPHER. *(swallows the water)* You cut my cheek.

BRIAN. You'll recover.

CHRISTOPHER. It hurts.

BRIAN. Listen to him. The street is full of cops out there who want to cut me in half. The smart ass over here has a croaker with a knife waiting for her and you're whining about your cut cheek . What am I supposed to do, say I'm sorry? O.K. I'm sorry.

(taps his own head with the gun)

It's no use. I can't think. Anyone got a suggestion besides suicide?

MADDY. Give it up. I know how you feel about doing time but some hope is better than nothing.

*(***BRIAN*** *looks at* ***CHRISTOPHER.*** *)*

CHRISTOPHER. The problem is beyond my fantasy. I get my dreams from books. I don't have any of my own. Reading is my meditation.

BRIAN. *(to* ***BETTY****)* And you? You've been giving me advice and smart cracks all along.

BETTY. Hell, I told you I'd probably panic at the door and give up. I haven't got the will. I'm no explorer, no undiscovered countries for me.

BRIAN. And that's it? I go out a nothing. Nothing.

BETTY. I don't know. You've given us the most exciting morning of the week. Of course, it's only Wednesday.

BRIAN. *(shrugging, smiles, looks at her with admiration)* You never give up.

BETTY. I don't do gentle. Maybe I should learn.

BRIAN. *(gets up, stretches, tucks the bag under his arm, checks the gun, tucks it in his belt, goes to the door, kicks the chair out of the way, gives them a Jimmy Cagney wave and as he walks onto the street says:)*

Be seeing you.

BETTY. *(takes a step toward him, changes her mind and allows him his moment)* See you.

*(***BRIAN*** *goes out the door.* ***CHRISTOPHER*** *hurries to the window to watch.* ***BETTY*** *turns away. Gunshots nearby. A roar. The bookstore window breaks and a bullet hits the coffee pot.* ***BRIAN*** *comes flying back into the store and hits the floor with* ***MADDY*** *and* ***CHRISTOPHER****, kicking*

the door closed behind him.)

BRIAN. Some crazy asshole took a shot at me. I was going to throw the gun but they started shooting. They could have killed me for Chrissake.

BETTY. *(who has not ducked for cover and is calmly drinking coffee)* I think that was the idea.

(The phone rings.)

You want me to get that?

*(**BRIAN** crawls over to the phone and takes it from **BETTY** who is still standing.)*

BRIAN. You know you could have killed me. I was just gonna throw the gun…Who?…There's a war going on here. What do you want?

(holds the phone away from him and looks around)

Some guy named Berg. Wants to know if you picked up the Dickens set.

MADDY. *(cowering near the window)* Tell him yes. He can pick it up tomorrow.

BRIAN. You can pick it up tomorrow…I don't know. Are you deaf or something? The cops are here shooting the place…*(removes phone from his ear)* He wants to know how much.

MADDY. Tell him thirty-five for the whole set.

BRIAN. Thirty-five for the set. Now get off the phone. I'm expecting a call. Life or death. *(sighs, puts the phone away again)* Nobody listens. He says he can only go thirty-two.

MADDY. He does that every time. We set the price.

BRIAN. I'll pay the three bucks extra. I'll pay a thousand. *(on phone:)* You got a deal, Berg. Goodbye.

*(He hangs up. The phone rings again. **BRIAN** picks it up.)*
Hello…It was some guy wanting to buy books. This is a bookstore. What the hell did you guys shoot at me for? I was coming out…No…I don't trust you…Will you stop using that word…There aren't any hostages

in here…They can go whenever they want…Now what are you gonna do to convince me I won't get blown away if I go out that door again?…No, no. That's not good enough. I think you guys want some headlines or something. Is there an election coming up around here?…I want some more time to think…Five or six more minutes. No, I don't want to talk to Eddie. That's what got me here in the first place. No, thank you very much. Goodbye. *(He hangs up and hands the phone to* **BETTY**.*)* You guys want to go on, go on. Go.

BETTY. If we go, they'll come in here shooting.

MADDY. They'll destroy the store, the books.

CHRISTOPHER. I'm just a customer and not a friend of the future deceased. I'm going.

MADDY. *(to* **BETTY***)* If you stay, I'm staying.

BETTY. There's no point in more than one of us staying and I've got the least to lose.

MADDY. They won't shoot if we're in here.

BRIAN. I can't take this. Go or stay, but make up your minds.

CHRISTOPHER. *(getting up carefully, he walks to the door)* If you go out with us, they won't shoot.

BRIAN. You want to bet your life on that.

CHRISTOPHER. Goodbye. I'll be back tomorrow if… Goodbye.

(And out he goes, hands in the air. There is a beat as the three remaining in the store listen for shots. From outside. A shout.)

I'm one of the hostages. Don't shoot.

BRIAN. *(getting to his knees, angrily, shouts after him)* You son of a bitch. There aren't any hos…Shit, what's the use.

MADDY. So, what do we do now?

BRIAN. It's their move.

BETTY. That's a comfortable plan. I'd offer you coffee, but the pot has been shot all to hell.

BRIAN. *(brightly, an idea)* Hey, what about this? I threaten to burn the money. Maybe I burn a few bills to prove I mean business. I tell them I'll burn it all unless they send me a public defender to guarantee that I'll get out of here alive.

BETTY. A few minutes ago you were talking about going out like Bonnie and Clyde.

BRIAN. That was before they shot at me. Now I'm talking about staying alive. How do I tell them? They didn't give me a number to call.

(The phone rings.)

BRIAN. *(answering it)* Yeah? No…no…no…Here's my deal. Take it or leave it. I start burning this money bill by bill till an unarmed cop comes and leads me out. You rush the place and I burn it in a pile. Right…right… bastard.

(He hangs up.)

Burn it. It ain't mine, the guy says. I'll show them I mean what I say.

(He pulls some bills out of the YMCA bag and goes to the window. Shouting out:)

I'm burning. See. You don't care. I don't care.

(He burns a bill and holds it up. The phone rings again. **BRIAN** *crawls to it, picks it up.)*

Yeah…Sure…Screw you…I'm burning it up, one bill at a time till you send someone here to lead me out. I figure I've got enough money in here for maybe four, five hours.

(He hangs up.)

Money talks.

(He crawls over and burns another bill.)

BETTY. And what happens when you burn up all the bills?

BRIAN. How the hell do I know? I'll burn books.

MADDY. The police don't care if you burn books.

BRIAN. I'll think of something. I'm on a streak here. You see? I've got an idea. It's something to do, to run with.

MADDY. *(panicking)* Let's play the first line game. "You don't know me without you have read a book by… "

BETTY. *The Adventures of Huckleberry Finn.* "Mrs. Ferrars died on the night of the 16th-17th September – a Thursday."

VOICE. *(from outside the window) The Murder of Roger Ackroyd.* Don't shoot.

BRIAN. *(pulls out his gun and fires a shot toward the voice)* Don't come in here.

(BRIAN looks around in panic and throws the YMCA bag over the counter out of sight.)

VOICE. Let me in here. Stop shooting. I'm supposed to get you out, not get me killed. You start shooting. They start shooting and I'll be dead.

BETTY. Come in.

(BRIAN gives her an angry look and then turns his gun trained on the broken window through which a CLOWN climbs.)

BRIAN. What the fuck is this?

MADDY. A clown.

BRIAN. I know it's a clown. What are they sending in a clown for. They think this is some kind of joke here? My life is on the line and they're sending in clowns.

CLOWN. *(agreeing. He is most agreeable. He doesn't want to be shot.)* Ridiculous. I told them it was ridiculous. Those were my exact words. Couldn't agree with you more.

BRIAN. They don't take me seriously.

(shouting out the window)

Do they know what I can do in here?

CLOWN. They know. Can I sit down?

BETTY. Pick a chair.

(CLOWN circles around the angry, wary BRIAN, goes to the only chair and sits, a miserable spectacle.)

BRIAN. Who the hell are you? And don't tell me you're a clown.

CLOWN. I'm not a clown. I mean I am a clown right now but I'm not a professional clown. I'm an assistant public defender. This is my day off. I was at the Children's Hospital around the corner doing a show.

MADDY. A show?

CLOWN. On my days off I pick up some extra money doing a clown act for birthdays, things like that. Today was a benefit. I came out see what was happening and this Lieutenant volunteered me, didn't want to risk one of his own men. I should have said no. I...

BETTY. You asked for someone. They sent you a Public Defender.

BRIAN. They sent me a clown. Can you feature the head-lines? I'll be laying there dead and my name won't even be mentioned. Clown dies in shootout with Sav-ings and Loan robber. It was a rotten idea.

CLOWN. (*gets up with a sigh*) A rotten idea. That's what I told them. I'll go now and...

BRIAN. Sit down.

(**CLOWN** *sits.*)

BETTY. (*The phone rings.* **BRIAN** *looks at it, ignores it and tries to think.* **BETTY** *walks over an picks it up.*) Hello...I'm fine...She's fine...The clown is fine...Brian is not so fine...I'll ask him.

(*She puts her hand over the mouthpiece and addresses* **BRIAN**)

Are you coming out?

(**BRIAN** *waves her away.* **BETTY** *goes back to the call.*)

I think he's thinking. Either that or he's trying to keep some poor demon trapped in his skull...No, no...It was a kind of joke to help relieve the tension...I'll try not to...I'll tell him.

(*She hangs up.*)

They're giving you ten more minutes.

MADDY. And then?

BETTY. They didn't say.

CLOWN. And then they'll give you ten more until you work things out.

BRIAN. Shut up. Stop it. I'm losing control again.

(He gets up and paces around the room waving his gun.)

This is a dream, a shitty dream.

CLOWN. You've got a point there.

BRIAN. *(stopping)* But it's no dream.

CLOWN. *(quick to agree)* No dream. You're right.

BRIAN. What's your name?

CLOWN. My name?

BETTY. He likes to know his victims names. It keeps them in line.

MADDY. He read it in a book.

CLOWN. My name is Buffo.

BRIAN. Your first name?

CLOWN. Roger.

BRIAN. Roger Buffo.

CLOWN. Roger Edmonds. I'm Buffo the Clown. I didn't know which you wanted, my real name or…

BRIAN. And you're supposed to lead me out?

(CLOWN nods glumly.)

I think they'll shoot us both if we go out there.

(CLOWN nods glumly.)

MADDY. *(looking out window)* Look at that. It's the Channel 4 News truck.

(Everyone but BRIAN looks.)

BETTY. You can go out now. They wouldn't shoot you unarmed in front of a television crew.

CLOWN. She's right.

MADDY. Just throw your gun out and walk out with your hands up.

BRIAN. *(rocks on the floor, undecided.)* It's such a…a nothing thing…a clown.

CLOWN. *(sinking into depression)* I don't know. I tried to do something good, cheer up sick kids polish my act, make a few extra dollars here and there. You think I couldn't make more in private practice than as a public defender?

BETTY. No, I don't think you could.

CLOWN. Maybe not. I am, to tell the truth, a lousy public defender. The police don't even hate me. They like me. They're happy when I'm defending.

BRIAN. If I make it alive, do I have to have you defend me?

CLOWN. I don't think so. Maybe. It depends on who they assign. I'd do my best.

MADDY. Which is…

CLOWN. None too good. But I'm a hell of a clown.

BETTY. Do something funny.

CLOWN. Adults don't find me funny

MADDY. Kids do?

    (CLOWN shrugs.)

CLOWN. I'm working on it.

    (The phone rings. BRIAN decides to get it. Speaks into the phone.)

BRIAN. I'll make a deal…What?…Berg, get off the phone… Off the phone you son-of-a-bitch…*(holding it away from him)* It's that Berg guy, says he's thought it over and will only go thirty for the Dickens set…*(into the phone)* Berg. Listen to this. *(fires the gun near the mouthpiece)* You hear that…*(shouting)* You'll be able to hear in a second…there's shooting death here Berg. No one gives a shit about Dickens…*(hangs up)*

(Phone rings again. **BRIAN** *picks it up.)*

Yes. Yes. Yes. O.K. I didn't shoot anybody. I just was making a point to some guy who called...About a set of Dickens...Oh shit. I'm gonna come out but I've got some conditions. *(He paces as he talks).* First, this clown in here is not going to be my public defender. O.K. I'll send him out before I go to talk to the television people so they can watch and see that I don't get blown away. I'll throw my gun out. Third, you let me take a book with me to the slam...What do you care?...It's by a nut case named Blake. You got a deal here or not?... O.K. *(He hangs up.)* Clown, you go out there. You tell the TV guys I'm coming out after I throw my gun. You can tell them everything, how I burned up the money, everything.

MADDY. How you... ?

BRIAN. Burned up every damned dollar.

CLOWN. I'll tell them.

BRIAN. Clown, get the hell out of here. You depress me.

CLOWN. *(get up agreeing)* It's a fact. We have that affect. Always have.

(goes to the door)

I'll do what I can out there for you.

*(***CLOWN*** *leaves.)*

*(***BRIAN*** *looks at* **BETTY** *and* **MADDY** *who return his look. They both smile.* **BETTY** *goes to a bin of books and starts looking at titles.)*

MADDY. *(makes a pile)* Self help books. Never thought much of them.

BRIAN. You find your own way or you don't get out.

(He strikes a match and starts a small fire. They watch it burn. **BRIAN** *reaches down and picks up the Blake book.)*

How much you charging for this?

BETTY. What you think is a fair price?

BRIAN. I don't know much about books. About sixty

thousand bucks seem fair to you?

BETTY. *(shrugging)* Close enough.

BRIAN. You'll find it back there.

(nods over at the back of the counter)

You might want to put it away before the cops come swarming in here when I leave.

*(**MADDY** moves behind the counter, picks up the sack and goes into the back room. While she is gone, **BRIAN** smoothes back his hair, adjusts his jacket. **BETTY** nods her approval. **MADDY** returns.)*

MADDY. It's in the safe.

BRIAN. What do you think you can buy with sixty grand?

MADDY. Maybe a good doctor.

BRIAN. Well, I'm going.

(looks at the book in his hand)

If I like it, I'll order another one. Got any suggestions?

BETTY. Lots.

*(**BETTY** walks toward him, her hand out. He shakes it.)*

BRIAN. A guy deserves a little dignity.

BETTY. Blake couldn't have said it better.

*(**BRIAN** whirls, throws the gun out of the window and steps out of sight into the window where a roar of the crowd and beams of light greet him on his face. He has his moment in the spotlight. He shows his teeth, puts his hands up and walks out with pride and swagger.)*

BETTY. What are we going to do with it, the money?

MADDY. Do with it? The operation. You can go to Boston now and get that doctor...doctor...

BETTY. No operation.

MADDY. Betty. Come on. We don't...

BETTY. *(She is starting to straighten up.)* No. I mean I don't need one. Dr. Forbes' nurse said it was nothing, a lymph node from an infection.

MADDY. *(Confused)* But you said… ?

BETTY. What should I have said when I put down the phone? "Good news Bank Robber with a gun, I've just been told I won't die in a month or two?" He would have helped us celebrate.

MADDY. You faked it?

*(**BETTY** nods.)*

That was all an act to make him think you didn't care, to…

BETTY. Maybe save our lives. So, how do we spend the money? We fix up the store, new inventory, spend some on vacation. We've got enough for all of it and the American Book Association Meeting in Denver.

MADDY. But he, Brian, thinks…

BETTY. And you think we should disappoint him, take away his belief that he did something noble? Out the window he went with Blake under his arm and a dopey grin of pride a mile wide. He's going to jail with a fantasy and a good book.

MADDY. *(helping to pick up books)* And we're… .

BETTY. On our way to Bermuda for the winter. The bank gets its insurance and the police get a bank robber.

(looks out the window)

Here they come.

MADDY. I'm not sure how to play this.

BETTY. *(shrugs)* He didn't hurt us, seemed confused and a little pathetic, a decent enough victim of society. We were frightened, but thank god its over.

MADDY. *(picks up a book and nods in agreement)* Betty, this is Blake's poems. Brian took the wrong book. He must… he must have taken *Slave Girls of the Kalahari.*

*(As **COP** from first act carefully enters through the window.)*

BETTY. We owe him one.

(CURTAIN)

ACT II

Scene I

(Office in Police Headquarters. It is late at night. Perhaps there is a clock on the wall that shows us it is around 11 p.m. The office is simple, desk, and a couple of chairs in front of it. CLAUDIA GINGRICH enters singing something light, possibly the "Under the Sea" from The Little Mermaid or "Ten Happy Fingers" from The Five Thousand Fingers of Dr. T. Claudia, in her early 30's, is wearing a suit with a white blouse. The blouse is open a few buttons at the top and she is wearing a very colorful costume jewel necklace. Her hair is flowing. She is carrying a briefcase. Claudia looks around the room, opens a desk drawer and sweeps everything on top of the desk into it except for the telephone. She continues to sing as she opens her briefcase on the desk and begins arranging items on it. The first item is a pack of cigarettes. She opens it, takes one out, lights it as she continues to lay items out – a large bottle of Tylenol, a bag of potato chips, a thick folder, a bottle of mineral water and two glasses, a wrapped sandwich. She surveys her work, pleased and then pulls out a mirror and examines herself. She takes off the necklace, buttons the blouse to the top, ties back her hair and puts on a pair of round, dark-rimmed glasses. The phone on the desk rings. CLAUDIA picks it up.)

CLAUDIA. Give me…*(She looks at her watch.)* …another thirty seconds and send the first one in and another thirty seconds after that before you send in the second one… Thirty seconds.

(She hangs up and continues to sing or hum as she

surveys what she has done to be sure it is right. She smiles, satisfied, puts out her cigarette, dumps the ashes into a waste basket and returns the ash tray to the desk. There is a knock at the door. **CLAUDIA** *stops humming and adopts a very weary look. She checks it in the mirror. Dissatisfied, she alters it. Pleased, she smiles and shoves the mirror into the drawer before she says…)*

CLAUDIA. Come in.

(The door opens. **CLAUDIA** *now looking dead tired moves behind the desk as* **EDDIE** *enters.* **EDDIE** *is somewhere in his late forties or fifties. He is very nervous. He is wearing dark trousers and a blue denim prison shirt with a number on the back. He closes the door behind him and looks up at* **CLAUDIA** *who says nothing but points to one of the chairs in front of the desk.* **EDDIE** *opens his mouth to speak but* **CLAUDIA** *stops him with…)*

CLAUDIA. No, not a word, not a fragment of a word. Not a sigh, a sound. One word will cost you a year, give or take a few months.

*(***EDDIE** *sits in one of the chairs, defeated. Another knock at the door.* **CLAUDIA** *is seated now. She looks as if she has a bad headache.)*

Come in.

*(***BRIAN** *enters wearing the same clothes he wore in Act I. He spots* **EDDIE** *almost immediately and says…)*

BRIAN. Eddie.

*(***EDDIE** *starts to sigh, stops himself. He doesn't look at* **BRIAN**. **CLAUDIA**'*s hand is to her forehead. She reaches for the Tylenol.)*

CLAUDIA. The door.

BRIAN. Eddie, what the hell did you… ?

CLAUDIA. Close the door.

*(***BRIAN** *closes the door almost as an afterthought. He is focused on* **EDDIE**. **BRIAN** *advances on* **EDDIE**.)*

BRIAN. Answer me Eddie or we're in for serious conflagration.

CLAUDIA. Sit down.

(**BRIAN** *is paying no attention to her. He is now hovering over* **EDDIE** *who tries to meet his eyes.*)

You have five seconds to sit down. If you are not seated and quiet in five seconds, you will be dragged out of here and will not hear the offer which I will make, an offer, which will be made only once.

(**EDDIE** *is partially blocked from* **CLAUDIA** *view by* **BRIAN**. **EDDIE** *nods for* **BRIAN** *to sit down.* **BRIAN** *turns to glare at* **CLAUDIA** *who is not looking at him. She is too busy downing a Tylenol. She points at the chair.* **BRIAN** *postures for an instant, then sits, arms folded, defiant. When she finishes her Tylenol,* **CLAUDIA** *reaches for her chips.*)

CLAUDIA. My name is Claudia Gingrich. I am an attorney for the Second Federal Savings and Loan Company. Would you like an organic potato chip?

BRIAN. No.

(**EDDIE** *shakes his head no.*)

CLAUDIA. I have a headache. I have not slept for two nights and I want to go home.

BRIAN. Tell me about it.

(**CLAUDIA** *is now looking at the file before her.*)

CLAUDIA. I have no interest in sharing confidences with you. I have no interest in a prolonged conversation with you. Your record and your behavior demonstrate that you are a stupid man. I do not enjoy conversations with stupid people.

(**BRIAN** *starts to get out of the chair.*)

A stupid man. What semi-intelligent human who reads the newspapers or watches the nightly news would rob a Savings and Loan. You're lucky you even found one still open. A mom and pop video store would be a better bet.

BRIAN. We didn't do so badly.

(CLAUDIA *holds up a tape recorder she has concealed on her lap.*)

CLAUDIA. You've just confessed. I told you you were stupid.

BRIAN. Entrapment. I know my rights.

CLAUDIA. No, you do not know your rights. I repeat. You are stupid. Sit back down.

(BRIAN *reluctantly sits and reaches for the pack of cigarettes on the desk.* CLAUDIA *watches him, lets him reach for the matches. He is about to light up when she says emphatically…*)

No.

(BRIAN *pauses.*)

I suffer from migraine headaches. I'm on the verge of one now. I'm getting an aura. I smell prison food.

(CLAUDIA *picks up the phone as he lights up defiantly and drops the match on the floor.*)

CLAUDIA. *(on the phone)* Send in an officer and take…

(BRIAN *stands angrily and puts out the cigarette.*)

…never mind.

(*She hangs up.* BRIAN *glares at her, then at* EDDIE.)

BRIAN. There's supposed to be a good cop. You're the bad cop. There's supposed to be a good cop.

(CLAUDIA *sighs.*)

CLAUDIA. I'm not a cop. I'm a lawyer. Do your best for a few moments to control your stupidity.

BRIAN. O.K. O.K. That's fucking it. I'll show you… "Mordant." You know what "mordant" mean?

CLAUDIA. Ah, a vocabulary lesson from a criminal who caught clutching a copy of …

(*She checks her notes.*)

…"Slave Girls of the Kalahari."

BRIAN. I grabbed the wrong book. It was supposed to be Blake's poems.

"Mordant."

CLAUDIA. "Caustic." Do you know what caustic means?

(**BRIAN** *is flustered but determined to see it through.*)

BRIAN. Mordant.

CLAUDIA. You're stupid. If you can simply accept that fact, we can get on with our business here and I can go home.

(**BRIAN** *won't give up.*)

BRIAN. "Gimmel."

CLAUDIA. *(wearily)* Either you are uttering the third letter of the Hebrew alphabet or you are mispronouncing a noun which means any of various joints for transmitting motion between moving parts. I find it difficult to imagine your having use for either word. One can be educated and still stupid. Look around you. Would you be here if you weren't stupid?

(**BRIAN** *suddenly turns and punches* **EDDIE** *who goes tumbling out of the chair and rises to his knees, his nose bloody. He opens his mouth to speak, but glances at* **CLAUDIA**. *She smiles at him and he stops.* **BRIAN** *turns to her but her smile is gone.*)

BRIAN. It was all his fault. His idea.

CLAUDIA. Gentlemen, and I use that word only in the hope that it may create a minimal atmosphere of human intercourse…You understand that the word "intercourse" need not be sexual but…

BRIAN. I know.

(**BRIAN** *and* **EDDIE** *sit.* **BRIAN** *fishes a crumpled handkerchief from his pocket and hands it to* **EDDIE** *who puts it to his bloody nose.*)

Why do you keep calling me stupid?

CLAUDIA. Because it irritates you.

BRIAN. Why do you… ?

CLAUDIA. Because it gets your attention.

BRIAN. What do you want?

CLAUDIA. The money.

BRIAN. There isn't any money. I burned it.

(*CLAUDIA shakes her head, removes her glasses, rubs the bridge of her nose and rises.*)

CLAUDIA. Why?

BRIAN. I wanted to give the cops the finger.

(*She shakes her head no and looks at* **EDDIE** *who looks down.*)

O.K. I wanted to destroy the evidence.

CLAUDIA. It was a little late for that. You knew your partner had confessed.

(**EDDIE** *looks away.* **BRIAN** *glares at him as she continues.*)

And there were witnesses.

BRIAN. I'm stupid. Alright? You said it. You're right. I'm stupid.

CLAUDIA. You are stupid but you are not insane. Give the money back and the charge will be reduced, for both of you. Attempted robbery. We'll see it that neither of you serves time. Keep telling me you burned it and you'll be decorating a cell toilet at Christmas for at least twenty years.

BRIAN. If I did have the money, and I'm not saying I do mind you, what about the cops? The States Attorney? The... ?

CLAUDIA. You've got a witness.

(*She points to* **EDDIE.** **BRIAN** *laughs.*)

You'll just have to trust me.

BRIAN. (*looking at* **EDDIE**) I don't trust you. I don't think I trust anyone or anything anymore.

CLAUDIA. You may be stupid but you are educable. I have an idea.

(CLAUDIA picks up the phone and hits a number.)

Why don't the two of you go someplace quiet where you can talk this over, improve your vocabularies, swap secrets and meditate?

(She looks at her watch.)

Twenty minutes should be enough. Then I'm going home and I'm not coming back.

(on the phone)

I'm sending Rocky and Bullwinkle out. Will you give them some place private to talk?...Thank you.

(She hangs up, folds her arms and nods toward the door. BRIAN grabs EDDIE's arm and urges him up. BRIAN turns to CLAUDIA as if to speak.)

I'll send ornaments.

EDDIE. Can I say something now?

CLAUDIA & BRIAN. No.

(BRIAN shoves EDDIE to the door, opens it and pushes EDDIE out. BRIAN turns to give CLAUDIA a final look of defiance, but she is not looking. She is rubbing her aching head with her hand. Her eyes are closed in pain. BRIAN slams the door. A beat and CLAUDIA opens her eyes, smiles, lights a cigarette, begins to pack her things away as she hums or sings happily. She is, in fact, carried away by the whole thing. She pauses, looks around the room and says, to herself...)

CLAUDIA. God, I love being a lawyer.

(CURTAIN)

ACT III

(Book Haven Book Shop a little after one in the morning. The store is in total darkness. We see nothing for at least a minute. Then a sound at the door, someone is breaking in as quietly as they can. The door gives way and we see a figure silhouetted in the doorway. The bearer of the flashlight trips and lets out a grunt. Suddenly, the lights go on to reveal **CHRISTOPHER** *sitting on the counter, his arm coming back from the switch on the wall. Flashlight in hand,* **BRIAN** *sits nursing a bruised side.)*

CHRISTOPHER. It'll only hurt for a year or two. Then it will go away.

BRIAN. What the hell are you doing here?

*(***BRIAN** *looks around. The shop has been straightened up a bit. There are boards covering the broken windows. The boards have a stenciled message: Emergency Enclosures. The clock indicates the time.)*

CHRISTOPHER. *(looks at him and opens the book on his lap. He reads out loud:)* I was in a Printing house in Hell, and saw the method in which knowledge is transmitted from generation to generation. In the first chamber was a Dragon-Man, clearing away the rubbish from a cave's mouth; within, a number of Dragons were hollowing the cave. In the second chamber was a Viper folding round the the rock and the cave, and others adorning it with gold, silver and precious stones. In the third chamber was an Eagle with wings and feathers of air: he caused the inside of the cave to be infinite; around were numbers of Eagle-like men who built palaces in the immense cliffs. In the fourth chamber were Lions of flaming fire, raging around and melting the metals into living fluids. In the fifth chamber were Unnam'd forms, which cast the metals in the expanse. There they were receiv'd by Men who occupied the sixth chamber, and took the form of books and were arranged in libraries.

(CHRISTOPHER closes the book and throws it toward BRIAN. He brandishes it threateningly.)

You forgot your book.

BRIAN. *(Turns off his flashlight and limps with it toward CHRISTOPHER. He brandishes it threateningly.)* What are you doing here?

CHRISTOPHER. *(leaps down to put the counter between him and BRIAN)* Same thing you are.

BRIAN. Which is?

CHRISTOPHER. Not witches, something far less mysterious, the sack of gold. Guess my name and you can have it all for yourself.

BRIAN. You've been drinking or sniffing or something. You're on something.

CHRISTOPHER. *(circling around the counter, staying ahead of the limping BRIAN)* I'm on to something. You didn't burn that money. I was here. You didn't have time. When I saw the news I thought, Rumplestilskin – dammit, I gave away my name – I thought that man is not telling the truth. That bag of bills must still be in that store. He shoved it someplace and it can't be too hard to find.

BRIAN. I burned that money.

CHRISTOPHER. Right, and you just came back for the book. Well, you have it. Now off you go.

BRIAN. You can't keep running.

CHRISTOPHER. And you can? Let's make a deal. Fifty-fifty.

BRIAN. No deal.

CHRISTOPHER. Thirty-five, sixty-five. You don't have much choice.

BRIAN. I can't make a deal.

(He reaches out and grabs CHRISTOPHER's coat. He lets out a sound of triumph and starts reeling him in.)

BETTY. *(stepping out of the back room)* Let him go.

(BRIAN lets him go. CHRISTOPHER staggers back. Both men look at BETTY.)

BRIAN. *(still nursing his bruise)* Hey great. You're here. I need the money back.

BETTY. Why aren't' you in jail?

BRIAN. I made a deal. The cops believed I burned the money. The insurance lawyer for the Savings and Loan didn't believe it. She gave me a deal. I give the money back and she'll get me off on probation. I made the deal. She got a fast bond hearing, put up the whole thing and gave me till the morning to come up with the pile.

BETTY. That's a touching story.

BRIAN. It's the goddamn truth. I'm sorry. I want you to have your operation. Hell, maybe we can take a few thousand out. I can tell them I burned that. They just want their sixty grand back.

MADDY. *(stepping out of the back room)* One hundred and seventy-two thousand, eight hundred and fourteen dollars.

BRIAN. Sweet Jesus. The lying b...I'm sorry.

BETTY. Nothing to be sorry about.

BRIAN. No, I'm sorry I have to take it back. Hell, with all that you can keep three, four thousand.

BETTY. No.

BRIAN. I want you to have it.

BETTY. There is no money. You burned it.

BRIAN. *(It sinks in.)* That's the way it is.

MADDY. We can't... .

BETTY. Oh, yes we can.

BRIAN. I'll tell them I gave it to you.

BETTY. We'll tell them we saw you burn it.

CHRISTOPHER. Right, we saw you burn it.

BETTY. *(to **CHRISTOPHER**)* You can leave, now.

CHRISTOPHER. But first a balm in Gilead or the promise thereof.

BETTY. There is no balm. The money is burned.

CHRISTOPHER. We won't accept that.

BRIAN. "'We?' What the hell are you talking, 'We,' Weasel Turd?"

(to BETTY*)*

Now I'm getting mad. Sick or no sick I want that money or I'll make you wish you were in surgery right now.

BETTY. *(She pulls a gun from under counter and aims it at* BRIAN *who backs up.)* I suppose if I just pull like on television it will go off. Intruder, middle of night, bank robber, back to the scene of the crime, whatever.

MADDY. No, for Chrissake, Betty. I don't want it like this.

CHRISTOPHER. Maybe we have room to negotiate here.

BETTY. *(wavers,* BRIAN *has put the book in front of him to ward off the feared bullet)* I don't see how.

(Sound at the door. Someone is trying to get in. They all look at each other)

BRIAN. Cops, checking.

*(*BETTY *reaches back and turns off the light. A beat and then the door opens slowly, creaking. Another silhouette appears and closes the door. A loud crash as the new member of the group crashes and thrashes about.* MADDY *turns on the light and they all face the new figure crumpled over a bin. He is in his thirties, not a very imposing figure, wearing a windbreaker, sweater, and white shirt with jeans.)*

ROGER. Oh, God that hurts a lot. I think I broke my knuckle.

BETTY. Who are you?

ROGER. *(Looks up.)* Me? I just came in to ask for directions. I'm lost and… .

MADDY. That voice. I know that voice.

ROGER. Voice. Right, lots of people think I sound like Bart Simpson.

(imitates Bart Simpson.)

Don't have a cow, man.

MADDY. The clown.

BRIAN. *(tt clicks)* Right. The clown. You're Sucko.

ROGER. Buffo. It's Buffo.

BETTY. And you were just out for a walk and happened to

stumble back here to relive this morning's stimulating experience?

ROGER. Something like that...

(He stands up, sees no one believes him.)

The money. He didn't burn it.

CHRISTOPHER. Right.

ROGER. Why? Hey, I'm a clown, but I'm not a fool.

CHRISTOPHER. Glenn Ford said something like that in Trial. I think it was "I can be fooled, but I'm no fool."

BRIAN. *(to BETTY)* O.K. Let's cut out the horse shit. Put the gun away. You're not gonna shoot us all. There's no story you could come up with that would make sense.

CHRISTOPHER. I don't know about that. You could...

(look from BRIAN)

No story at all.

BETTY. *(gun still up, to ROGER)* You have a family?

ROGER. Wife and three kids...no, four kids. Make that four kids.

BRIAN. You're lying.

ROGER. A little.

MADDY. We can't stand here all night. Someone come up with something.

CHRISTOPHER. We share.

BRIAN. No way we share. I have to turn all that in or I get sent up.

BETTY. You deserve to get sent up. You committed armed robbery. What kind of a damned world is it anyway where robbers can make deals with banks? What about the people you could have killed? What about what you did here?

ROGER. Actually, it was a Savings and Loan, but it's not unusual for deals to be made with banks or insurance companies. I lost a case a few weeks ago in...

MADDY. No. The money has to go back.

CHRISTOPHER. That's undemocratic. We didn't vote.

MADDY. This isn't a democracy.

ROGER. It's not really my business, though I guess in a way it is my business now. I mean not professionally but... but... as an interested party.

BETTY. Make your point.

ROGER. You can't keep that money unless we cooperate and we don't cooperate unless we get a share.

BRIAN. What's the matter here? You all deaf? No shares. We're talking about my life, going to the pen.

(*He grabs* **ROGER** *and shakes him.*)

I've had enough lawyers for one night. I'm talking about my life and you're talking about how much you get.

BETTY. (*lowers her gun slightly*) Maybe we can make a deal.

BRIAN. The only deal I can think is that I give you enough for your operation and I walk out of here with the sack and that's a deal.

BETTY. I don't need an operation.

CHRISTOPHER. You don't...Hey, that's great news.

BRIAN. Wait. Wait. Wait.

(*His hands are in the air.*)

That was all an act, for me?

(**BETTY** *nods.*)

That does it. You get nothing.

BETTY. (*hand comes up and the gun points at* **BRIAN**) There are two things we can do here. We can give the robber his money and let him walk out, or we can shoot him and divide it four ways.

MADDY. No.

CHRISTOPHER. Seems fair to me.

ROGER. I want a few seconds to think about that.

MADDY. Why can't we just insist that he burned it? It's all of our words against his.

ROGER. Too many questions if he keeps claiming he didn't burn it. They'll watch you, search. One of us will break.

(*Silence.* **BRIAN** *looks around at them, at* **MADDY**.)

BRIAN. Hey, wait a minute here. You're all sitting around deciding to kill me.

ROGER. Looks that way.

MADDY. Are you going to shoot me, too?

BETTY. No, but once he's gone I don't see that you'll have much choice. He'll be dead and we'll have the money. If you turn us in, no money and we'll all go to jail.

ROGER. At least.

BRIAN. There's a death penalty in this state.

ROGER. He's right.

CHRISTOPHER. That's never been a deterrent in the past. I don't see why it should affect this situation.

BRIAN. What a group. Never in my life, and it's been down more than up, have I ever even given serious thought to icing someone, never. Well, maybe once when Phil and Wass gave me…but I didn't do it. And look at you here? Look at you? I give up. Keep the money. I'll go to jail.

(He turns to leave.)

BETTY. Hold it. That won't work.

ROGER. Right. We can't really take your word. You're a convicted felon, an armed robber whose life is at stake. You'll go out that door and find the nearest policeman.

BRIAN. No, I won't.

ROGER. Yes, you will.

BRIAN. No, I won't.

BETTY. Stop it. It'll be done.

(She raises her hand, aims at **BRIAN**. **MADDY** *reaches back and turns off the light. There is a gunshot. Some-one screams. Shuffling. The door opens. A figure is silhouetted against it.)*

Take another step and I'll shoot again.

(The figure backs into the room. Lights go on. **BRIAN** *is standing with his hands up.* **MADDY, BETTY, CHRIS-TOPHER, ROGER** *all look at each other, and* **MADDY** *collapses.)*

CHRISTOPHER. She's hurt.

BRIAN. *(with angry sarcasm looking at the horrified* **BETTY***)* She's shot.

BETTY. *(drops the gun, reaches for* **MADDY***.)* Get a doctor. Get a doctor.

CHRISTOPHER. I went to medical school for a year.

(He goes to **MADDY.** **BRIAN** *puts his arms down, folds them and leans against the wall.* **ROGER** *backs away from him toward the door.* **BRIAN** *cuts him off and* **ROGER** *returns to the center of the room.* **CHRISTOPHER** *looks at* **MADDY** *who is groaning.)*

Blood. I hate blood. That's why I didn't finish medical school. I don't think it's too bad, but she needs a doctor. Stop the bleeding.

(He turns his head away. **BRIAN** *goes behind the counter, into the washroom and returns with a towel. He gives it to* **BETTY** *who takes it and stops the bleeding as best she can.)*

BETTY. Maddy, I'm sorry. Why did you… ?

ROGER. Gun control. I've been telling kids about handguns for…

(a look from **BRIAN** *wilts him.)*

BRIAN. *(examines* **MADDY***)* I think she'll be all right. Now, how about I just get my money and walk out of here? Unless you plan on shooting your friend a few more times.

BETTY. *(searches for the gun)* Damn you, you…

BRIAN. *(backing away from the book she throws at him)* Lady, you got more balls than a pool table. You'd have made a hell of a robber and that's a fact. Tell you what I'll do. You can have ten grand. Ten. The insurance people can take it or leave it.

BETTY. You'll tell.

BRIAN. I won't

CHRISTOPHER. He'll tell.

ROGER. You can't trust a man in his position.

BETTY. *(still cradling the moaning* **MADDY,** *she looks at* **BRIAN.)** He won't tell.

(to **CHRISTOPHER***)*

Call the ambulance, damn you.

*(***CHRISTOPHER** *picks up the phone, calls moving behind the counter.)*

In the safe back there. Combination is 27 left, 35 right, 16 left.

*(***BRIAN** *hurries into the washroom.)*

CHRISTOPHER. *(on phone.)* Right. An accident. We thought we saw a burglar and the gun went off.

(He hangs up.)

They'll be right here.

MADDY. Betty, he shot me.

BETTY. No, Maddy. I shot you.

MADDY. You shot me? I don't understand.

BETTY. I don't either. The ambulance will be here in a few minutes.

ROGER. I think I'll be going.

BETTY. You do that.

BRIAN. *(comes back with the Y.M.C.A. bag)* How's she look?

BETTY. I don't know.

BRIAN. I left a stack of bills in the safe and locked it.

BETTY. Thanks.

CHRISTOPHER. I think the police would like to know about that pile of bills.

ROGER. *(right behind him)* I think they would.

BRIAN. *(takes* **BETTY***'s gun)* If they find out, there is going to be two dead clowns on the street.

CHRISTOPHER. Then again, they may not find that out.

ROGER. Probably won't.

BRIAN. Get going, ahead of me.

*(***ROGER** *and* **CHRISTOPHER** *move to the door, when* **BRIAN** *turns to talk to* **BETTY,** *and* **CHRISTOPHER** *heists a few books.)*

BRIAN. No hard feelings.

BETTY. No. And you?

> (**BRIAN** *motions to* **CHRISTOPHER** *and* **ROGER** *who leave. An ambulance siren is heard in the distance.* **BRIAN** *holds up the book.*)

BRIAN. I got the right book this time. See you around. It's been a predacious experience.

> (*He exits.*)

MADDY. Betty, my back hurts.

BETTY. Hold still. The ambulance is coming. I can hear them. You're not hurt badly.

MADDY. Did you shoot him?

BETTY. No, Maddy, I shot you.

MADDY. Oh. Did he get the money?

BETTY. Most of it. He left us a few thousand in the safe.

MADDY. No.

BETTY. He didn't leave us a few thousand?

MADDY. Under the counter, in the box for Mr. Berg, with the Dickens. I put thirty thousand in there.

BETTY. Thirty…

MADDY. Oh…Betty do something, anything. Let's play the game till they get here.

BETTY. (*looks in the air, thinking, and then, as we hear an ambulance siren in the distance and the lights go down*)
"Once an angry man dragged his father along the ground through his own orchard."

MADDY. Gertrude Stein, *The Making of America.*

BETTY. Let me finish. "Stop? cried the groaning old man at last. Stop? I did not drag my father beyond this tree."

MADDY. (*with a small groan.*) Another.

BETTY. "They endured."

MADDY. Faulkner, *The Sound and the Fury.* But that's not a first line, Betty. It's the last line.

BETTY. I know Maddy. I know.

> (*The siren grows close and loud. The lights go down.*)

> (*CURTAIN*)

STUART KAMINSKY is author of 50 published novels, 5 biographies, 4 textbooks and 35 short stories. He also has screenwriting credits on four produced films including *Once Upon a Time In America, Enemy Territory, A Woman In The Wind* and *Hidden Fears.* He is a past president of the Mystery Writers of America and has been nominated for six prestigious Edgar Allen Poe Awards including one for his short story "Snow" in 1999. He won an Edgar for his novel *A Cold Red Sunrise,* which was also awarded the Prix De Roman D'Aventure of France. He has been nominated for both a Shamus Award and a McCavity Readers Choice Award. Kaminsky writes several popular series including those featuring Lew Fonesca, Abraham Lieberman, Inspector Porfiry Petrovich Rostnikov, and Toby Peters. He has also written two original Rockford Files novels. He is the 50th annual recipient of the Grandmaster 2006 for Lifetime Achievement from the Mystery Writers of America.

Other plays by **STUART KAMINSKY**

The Final Toast

Please visit our website **samuelfrench.com** for complete descriptions and licensing information